Good-bye, Curtis

BY **KEVIN HENKES**

PICTURES BY **MARISABINA RUSSO**

Greenwillow Books, New York

Gouache paints were used for the full-color art. The text type is Swiss 721.

Manufactured in China by South China Printing Company Ltd.
First Edition   10 11 12 13 SCP 20 19 18 17 16 15 14

Library of Congress Cataloging-in-Publication Data

Henkes, Kevin.
Good-bye, Curtis / by Kevin Henkes ; pictures by Marisabina Russo.
p. cm.
Summary: Everyone in the neighborhood says a fond farewell to
Curtis, their beloved longtime letter carrier, on his last day of work.
ISBN 0-688-12827-0 (trade).   ISBN 0-688-12828-9 (lib. bdg.)
[1. Postal service—Letter carriers—Fiction.]
I. Russo, Marisabina, ill.   II. Title.
PZ7.H389Go   1995   [E]—dc20
94-19368   CIP   AC

For Dad and Mom
—K. H.

For Eunice and Whitney
—M. R.

Curtis has been a letter carrier

for forty-two years.

Today is his last day.

Everyone loves Curtis—

the old woman on the hill,

the baby in 4-C,

the clerk at the butcher shop,

and the crossing guard

at the corner of First and Park.

TODAY'S SPECIALS
Boneless steaks   3.98
Boneless Pork chops   3.99
Pork Tenderloin Filets 4.99
Chicken Legs   .79
Turkey Breast   5.99

STOP

All of the mailboxes all over his route

are filled with all kinds of surprises.

There is a chocolate cupcake

with sprinkles

from Mrs. Martin.

There is a drawing

from Debbie, Dennis,

and Donny.

There is a bottle

of aftershave

from the Johnsons,

and a box of nuts

from their dog.

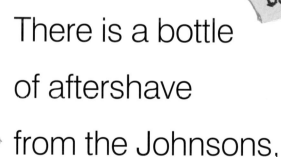

There are cards

and candy

and cookies.

There are

hugs

and handshakes

and kisses.

There is a small,

fat book

from Mr. Porter,

and a pencil sharpener

in the shape of

a mailbox from Max.

Boneless steaks   3.98
Boneless Pork Chops   3.99
Pork Tenderloin Filets 4.98
Chicken Legs   .79
Turkey Breast   5.19

"We'll miss you, Curtis,"

say the old woman on the hill

and the baby in 4-C

and the clerk at the butcher shop

and the crossing guard

at the corner of First and Park.

The children

Curtis met

when he first began his route

have grown up.

Some of them have children

of their own.

Some of them

have grandchildren.

Some of the children
have had dogs.
Some of the dogs
have had puppies.
Cats have had kittens, too.

Trees have grown from little to big.

Houses have been torn down.
And houses
have gone up.

People have moved out.
And people have moved in.

But everyone loves Curtis.

"We'll miss you," they all say.

The dogs and cats say so, too.

When Curtis gets to the last

mailbox at the last house

on the last street . . .

SURPRISE! SURPRISE! SURPRISE!

Curtis's own family is waiting there.

Friends pour out the door and

down the steps.

People from all over his route

run out from the backyard.

They have a party in Curtis's honor.

"We love you, Curtis," they all say.

"We'll miss you."

There is dancing and eating and
remembering. There are balloons
and streamers and tiny tin horns.

That night Curtis dreams of his party.
When he wakes up the next morning,
he begins writing thank-you notes
to everyone.
And he knows all the addresses
by heart.